DOUG T

A Working Dog's Tale

Cate Archer

5m

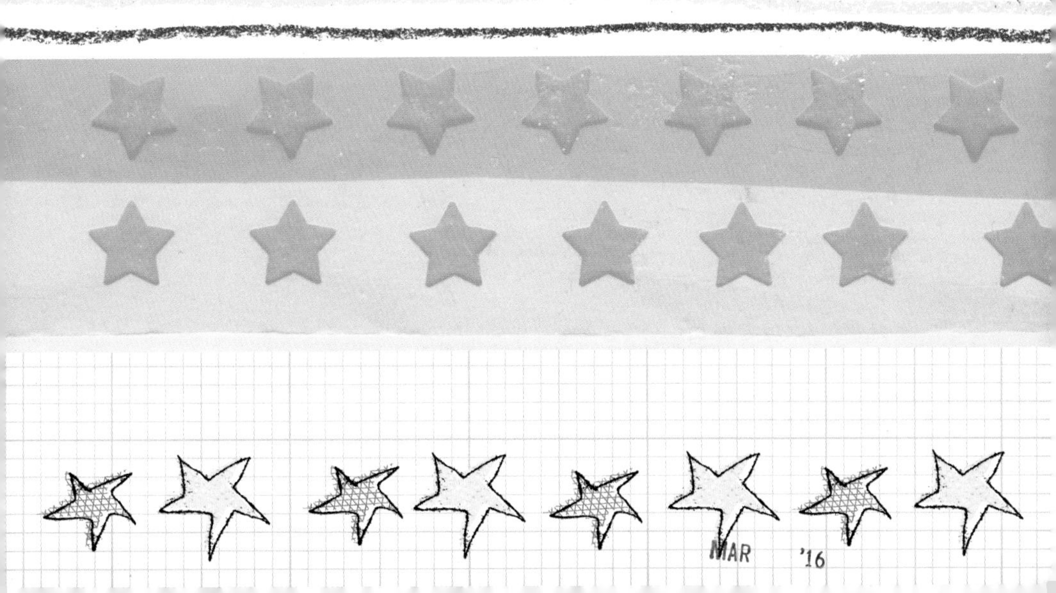

First published 2016

Published by
5M Publishing Ltd,
Benchmark House,
8 Smithy Wood Drive,
Sheffield, S35 1QN, UK
Tel: +44 (0) 1234 81 81 80
www.5mpublishing.com

A Catalogue record for this book is available from the British Library

ISBN 978-1-910455-15-9

Book layout by Alice Palace
Printed by Replika Press Pvt Ltd, India
Photographs by Cate Archer
Graphic design by Alice Palace

Contents

Doug the Pug – A Working Dog's Tale

Foreword

PETS AS THERAPY

Clare Charity Centre, Wycombe Road, Saunderton, High Wycombe, Bucks HP14 4BF
Tel. 01844 345445 www.petsastherapy.org

At Pets As Therapy, we are delighted that Doug the Pug has chosen to support and promote all that we value and hold so dear. We are very proud of our national charity that helps Doug, and other gentle dogs like him, do such great work throughout the UK.

Scientists now recognise the very special bond that exists between us and our companion animals and how this supports us throughout life in so many different ways. The significant health and social benefits, associated with having animals as companions, are found to give us a respect and value for all life.

Pets As Therapy currently has nearly 5,000 registered volunteers visiting hospitals, hospices, nursing and care homes, schools and other venues with their dogs. All of these dogs have been assessed to ensure that they are of a suitable and predictable temperament.

There are many people who benefit from the particular brand of care, companionship and therapy we provide through our animals. Under clinical supervision, we are increasingly being asked to participate in assisting with phobias, stroke rehabilitation and those who have very severe sensory or physical disabilities or mental health problems.

In 2011, Pets As Therapy launched the incredibly popular READ2DOGS programme that Doug and his young friends particularly enjoy.

PETS AS THERAPY

Clare Charity Centre, Wycombe Road, Saunderton, High Wycombe, Bucks HP14 4BF
Tel. 01844 345445 www.petsastherapy.org

Many schools, requiring our services, remain on our waiting list as we seek more volunteers and every year some of our pets retire – so it is important that new pets and their owners are encouraged to continue this good work. Each and every one of Doug's books purchased will help us in this quest – all royalties from "Doug the Pug – A Working Dog's Tale" have been donated to Pets As Therapy.

Doug's great tale really touches me and he makes such a strong stand for people who may feel different. I think so many children will love Doug's story and understand Doug's message to be yourself and value and respect your relationships with other people. The discussions page at the end of the story will help to share further learning and understanding.

I hope you enjoy reading Doug's journey. After meeting Doug I realised he's everything the book says he is and a very inspirational chap. I'm sure this tale will inspire people who may have wonderful dogs at home to read this and feel "I could be a part of that"!

Thank you

Anne Clilverd
SEN (MH) RMN
Chair, Pets As Therapy

Introduction

"Doug The Pug – A Working Dog's Tale" is a book for children. It's also for those who enjoy reading with them. Pug lovers might like it too. In fact, I'd like to think that anyone interested in the beautiful relationship we have with our companion animals might like it. Even those who don't think a Pug is a proper dog might like it! Doug IS a proper dog! He is never seen peeping from a handbag – ever - but he does lounge around like a furry slug and does look rather more like a fat rabbit than a dog.

This sweet tale, highlighting the joys of the human/animal bond, is based on Doug's genuine working life through the UK charity Pets As Therapy. Its aim is to encourage us to be happy with who and what we are, celebrate each individual's differences and recognise that we all have something quite wonderful to offer.

When reading Doug's book, you will see that there is a glossary at the bottom of each page - this is to explain any tricky words that might be new to you. Those new words are all marked with a little paw print. Some writers put a glossary at the end of the book but I think that having it on each page makes it easier to keep track of where you are, and what it's all about, without losing your place.

At the end of Doug's story, there is a "Further Learning" section. You might like to read this to consider and reflect upon Doug's beliefs and values. Respecting and showing regard for the opinions of others is really important and often there are no right or wrong answers when talking about how we feel. In this section, you will also find ways to learn more about working animals and how they help us and how we can help them.

Doug and I wouldn't have such a lovely working life together if it wasn't for the great work of Pets As Therapy. So, I am delighted that Pets As Therapy will benefit from every one of Doug's books purchased.

I hope that through reading Doug's book, a greater understanding of companion animal therapy will be gained and funds raised may enable Pets As Therapy to further their good work.

I would be delighted if those with soppy predictable dogs at home were to read this and think, "I could do that"!

Sending you my warmest wishes, Cate

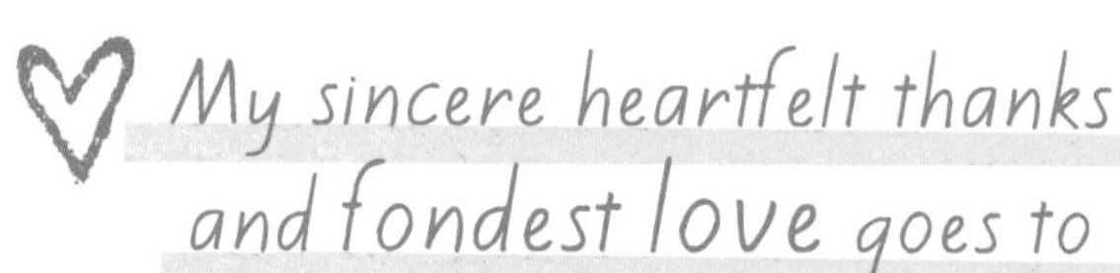

My daughter, Alice – without whom Doug the Pug would not have entered our lives or those he cares for in his noble work. Alice **truly believed** Doug would be **everything** he is. Without her, this book could never have been written. I **love** and **adore** her as she does me.

My son, James – for the tender hearted indulgence he shows both me and my work. I **love** him for this **MORE** than he can **ever** know. It was James who chose the **fabulous** name by which Doug the Pug is known and **loved** by so **many**.

My husband, Nick – who trusts and believes in **everything** I live and breathe. He encourages me to follow my **heart** and never doubts me. I **love** and cherish ALL he is to me.

My mother, Tottie – for making the time to share stories with me so patiently and **lovingly** from an early age, despite having such an incredibly busy life. She gave me my **love** of books and the tales they have within them. It has been a joy for me to share stories with my own lovely children and she gave me this gift.

And I would also like to thank, wholeheartedly,

Sarah Hulbert and Denise Power from 5m and Roger Smith and his wife Lesley - for being such good, kind and supportive friends in helping Doug's tale to be told.

The very clever Alice Palace - whose visual interpretation of my work gives Doug's tale warmth, life and vibrancy. To see more of Alice Palace's fabulous work, please look at her website www.alicepalace.co.uk where you will find all sorts of special creations that you might like to commission or purchase.

My lovely little **great** niece, Evie King - for being my wonderfully accommodating model and absolute superstar. She is also the **great** producer of our **fantastic** artwork on pages 28 & 29!

The lovely Lollipop Lady, Jo Walker, of Chalfont St Giles, for kindly seeing Doug and his young friends safely across the road and on their way to school.

The fabulous collection of Doug's good friends, below, for their modelling skills!

Milly, the Pug, Doug's special girlfriend
Ernie, the Black Labrador, our 'sniffer dog'
Nahla, the Golden Retriever, our 'guide dog'
Milo, the Designer Hybrid, our 'hearing dog'
Jess, the Collie, our 'sheep dog'
Killer, the Rottweiler, our 'guard dog'
Molly, our very own lovely Chocolate Labrador, she of longer legs. Doug's best friend, ever!
Bailey, the Lurcher/Labrador combo, our dog of longer nose
Scrappy, the Chihuahua, our dog of bigger ears
Aunt Agatha of Shropshire, Cocker Spaniel, she of longer ears
Doug's two cats, Tiger & Alfie.

Last, but not least, the wonderful philanthropist himself - Doug the Pug, so **rightly** loved, adored and respected for his benevolent approach to life!

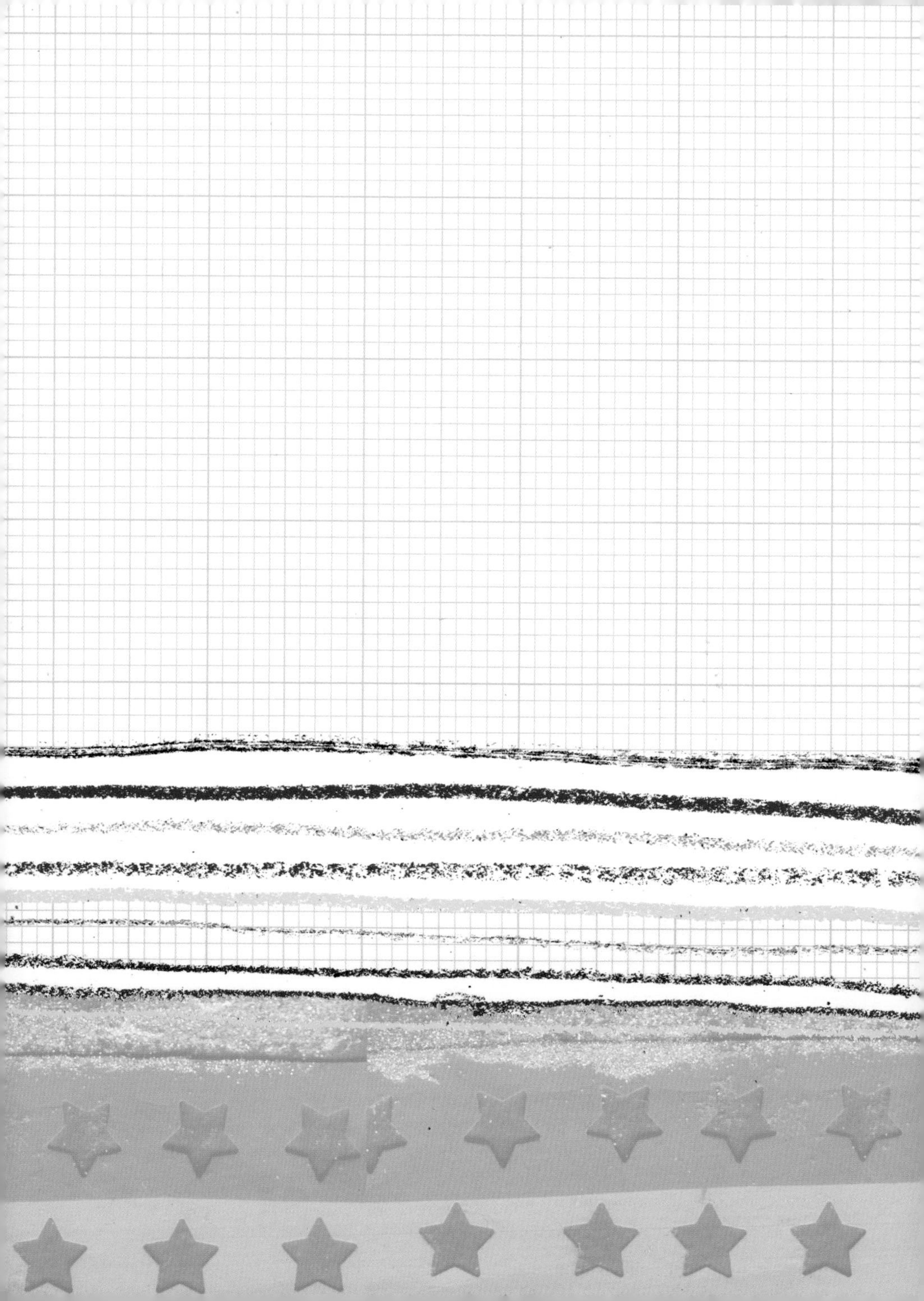

I dedicate this book

to

my late father,
Henry Brewis.

I miss you.

I wish you had been with
me to share this journey.

I know you would have been so very
proud of me and I know that you would
have found Doug quite ridiculous.

Doug's
story
starts
here

Doug the Pug is a Pug.

And a Pug is, in actual fact, a **perfectly WONDERFUL** breed of dog. Said to originate from China, as long ago as the 16th century, the Pug has been a **beloved** companion to **many** ever since.

breed = A particular type or kind of animal within a group of similar animals
originate = To start or come from
century = Period of 100 years

Apart from the **QUEEN** of course, who appears to hold a mystifying preference for her foxy Corgis, the Pug is a **particular** favourite of the royals (Kings and Queens), aristocrats (Lords, Ladies and other very posh people) and discerning commoners (those who make up the rest of us).

corgi = A breed of dog (that looks a little bit like a fox) and a favourite of Queen Elizabeth

discerning = Seeing things clearly and wisely

In fact almost everyone who has met a Pug finds them to be quite **adorable**. Pugs are said to eat into your **heart**. And **indeed** they do just that.

The Pug is **ridiculously** small for a dog. It has a particularly quizzical appearance and quite a peculiar scrunched-up face too. Some people think this makes our friend Doug the Pug look awfully cross. Though he never is. Never, ever.

Doug does, however, appear to be VERY confused. And confused he is. Doug **always** looks as if he's not quite sure what's going on in the world as we know it. It's as if he's been born **too** late - perhaps in the wrong era. He's rather a traditional sort and this does make him feel a little out of things at times.

era = Time in history

Like a square peg in a round hole, as some would say.

Doug does feel that he is now most true to himself but did once think it might be **cool** to be **cool**.

But, he is who he is and he's **happy** with that. And he likes to think that others feel happy with who they are too.

It may also be said that Doug can often appear somewhat bewildered. Totally and absolutely bewildered as to why people might want to be unkind to each other. Doug really has no comprehension as to what purpose this could possibly bring to anyone's life. He really **cannot** understand how anyone would want to make someone sad. Especially so, when it is such an **absolute JOY** to make someone **happy**. It can never quite be known what difficult times people are going through and a little kindness truly does **brighten** anyone's day. Even if it doesn't appear so, it **most certainly** does. Such kindness then ripples round to others rather like a tiny pebble dropping softly into a puddle.

Being rather earnest, Doug the Pug is both curious and scholarly. So, he does sometimes wonder from where the name "Pug" originates. Looking into this, and consulting a dictionary (as of course he would), Doug spots the word "Pug" and sees it defined as "a dog of small breed with a flat nose and wrinkled face". Rather miffed, Doug feels this is a totally inadequate description, perhaps even bordering on the dismissive.

bewildered = Baffled, totally mystified
earnest = Thoughtful and honest
curious = Eager to learn or know
scholarly = Interested in all things clever and educational
miffed = Mildly irritated
inadequate = Not enough

He seeks to look further and sees the word "pugnacious". This is understood to mean "aggressive", "antagonistic" and "quarrelsome". Surely not. This is CERTAINLY **not** an association one could ever link with Doug the Pug. If looking for just a single word to describe Doug accurately one could possibly even say "magnanimous" to be **more** apt.

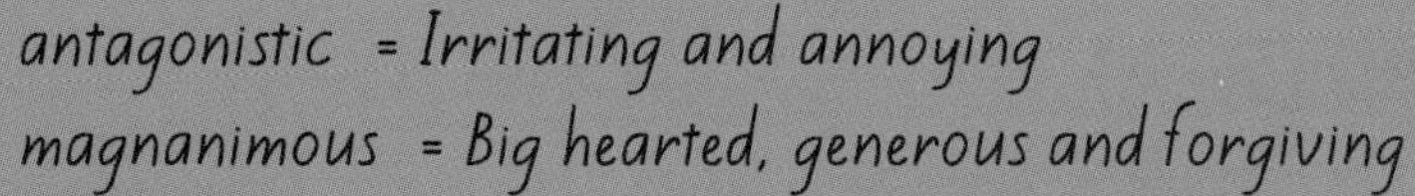

antagonistic = Irritating and annoying
magnanimous = Big hearted, generous and forgiving

Magnanimous he may be, we all know that nobody's quite perfect. Doug is really no exception to this rule. Almost perfect, but not quite. It is regrettable to say that Doug is renowned for being an **absolute** greedy scavenger. Ridiculously **greedy** in fact. This hankering for **more** and **more** food has, at times, caused him enormous grief.

Despite feeling the presence of his very own little Jiminy Cricket, sitting scornfully on his shoulder, Doug would sneak out, through the cat flap of all places, to pinch the cats' food.

renowned = Well known
scavenger = Searcher of things amongst rubbish or discarded things
hankering = Desperately seeking
Jiminy Cricket = Pinocchio's friend who acts as his conscience and teaches him to recognise right from wrong
scornfully = With great disapproval

He would do this even after he had just finished dinner of **his own**. Even when it had been locked, to prevent such dastardly behaviour, Doug discovered that he could ram raid the cat flap with his shoulder, to shake down the lock, in order to sneak out. As he was then eating not only his own food but that meant for others too, he became a little rotund. Actually **much more** than a little rotund. It was of no surprise then, to anyone at all but Doug, to find that he no longer fitted through the cat flap with such ease. Such continuing mischief resulted in Doug suffering a serious limb injury necessitating a whole month of having to be carried absolutely everywhere at **all** times. It must be said that this indulgent convalescence was enjoyed with a little **more** grace than is rightly **acceptable**.

dastardly = Not nice at all
ram raid = Crash against in order to break through
rotund = Rounded and plump
limb = Arm or leg
convalescence = Time given for recovery from illness or injury

Alas, we digress. We should return to Doug in his quest for the true meaning of the word "Pug" and whence it came.

So, Doug sees, when checking his dictionary once more, a word he cannot initially pronounce. He then sees that it is to be said as "pyoojilism" - despite being spelt "pugilism". Pugilism is said to be the practice of boxing with one's fists.

alas= Exclamation or expression of mild disappointment
digress = Move away from
quest = Search
whence = From where

This is something Doug would never do. But, funnily enough, there was once a famous African American boxer called Sugar Ray Robinson who has been cited as one of the greatest boxers of ALL time.

This news really is quite exciting for Doug the Pug to discover as he actually started life himself with the name of Sugar Ray. This is Doug's professional Kennel Club name but his family much prefers to call him Doug the Pug.

Although Doug the Pug does not necessarily condone such things as boxing, and therefore feels it is quite inappropriate and totally absurd to be named after a boxer, Sugar Ray Robinson was said to have had a flamboyant personality and striking good looks. He was charismatic and had a flair for the dramatic. That sounds much more like Doug. So, perhaps his breeder wasn't so wrong after all.

cited = Famously mentioned
Kennel Club = The governing body for dog activities in the United Kingdom and register of UK pedigree dogs
condone = To accept behaviour not really approved of
absurd = Silly
flamboyant = Theatrical
charismatic = Charming and appealing

And, fancy this, Sugar Ray Robinson was married to a **beautiful** girl called Milly. And, it just so happens, there is a rather fetching little apricot-coloured Pug called Milly living just around the corner from Doug. She is **the love** of Doug's life and he is utterly **devoted** to her.

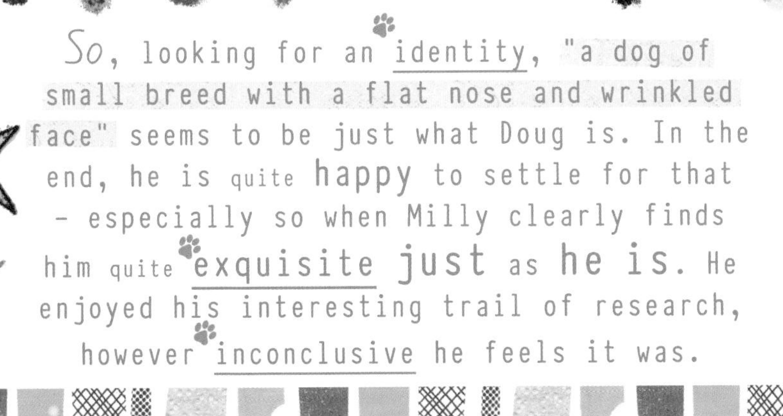

So, looking for an identity, "a dog of small breed with a flat nose and wrinkled face" seems to be just what Doug is. In the end, he is quite happy to settle for that - especially so when Milly clearly finds him quite exquisite just as he is. He enjoyed his interesting trail of research, however inconclusive he feels it was.

But Doug is rather chuffed to discover that Oscar Wilde, a 19th century author and poet, was once thought to have said "I sometimes think that God, in creating the Pug, somewhat underestimated his ability". Doug considers this statement to be both faithful and true to the Pug. And, also, as Oscar Wilde was well known for his dazzling style and glittering conversation, Doug reckons his judgement is as good as one can find.

identity = Who, or what, a person or thing is
exquisite = Very beautiful
inconclusive = Without useful ending

So, Doug lives every day with the true belief that he is a VERY special dog. And indeed he is (despite being a greedy scavenger). In fact he walks with the sort of trot most often seen on a smart dressage pony.

dressage = Skilful
combination of dance and walk illustrated by trained horses/ponies

His tail is **perfect** for a Pug. It has been described just like a double cinnamon twist (without the fragrance of such, naturally).

Doug, as we would expect, is **incredibly** WELL BRED and of a **VERY high** pedigree. He presumes to be treated as such too, though this is essentially at odds with his belief that we are all of equal importance. And, he is blissfully unaware that he has the tiniest tufty grey beard (on his otherwise perfectly defined chin) and ears which don't quite fold in the way that a Pug's ears should.

Doug believes that personal differences should actually be **celebrated**.

He is therefore VERY proud of his distinctive **individuality**. And so he should be.

cinnamon twist = Delicious sugary, spicy curled pastry
pedigree = From a family all of the same pure breed
distinctive = Particular

Doug the Pug enjoys a life of fine comforts. He likes to be warm and snug and strongly dislikes the rain. In fact, if it is raining, Doug insists that he is carried outside under a very LARGE golfing umbrella to ensure that he stays dry. If he had a jewelled velvet cushion on which to be carried it is thought he might be happier still.

Despite being **very** small, and having **incredibly** short legs, Doug actually runs like the wind. Though he does run rather more like a rabbit than a dog.

RUN WITH ME DOUG!

It is said that one must **never** judge by appearances and Doug is testament to such a philosophy. He looks particularly slothful, when in fact he is not; and he looks quite cross, when he is indeed **the sweetest** dog **ever** born.

despite = Even though
testament = Proof or evidence of something
philosophy = Study of beliefs
slothful = Slow moving like the sloth (a sleepy animal from America)

Doug feels he is **fortunate** to have **many** friends from ALL walks of life. He **particularly enjoys** the company of cats. And they love him too, despite him behaving like a scoundrel when pinching their leftovers. There is, however, a rather silly preconception that dogs should not be friendly with cats. Doug likes to show that he will **happily** choose his friends for himself, regardless of what other people say. **Quite right too.** But, Doug the Pug is not only a **most** faithful and loyal companion to many, he is also a Working Dog.

scoundrel = Someone who does dreadful things
preconception = An idea or opinion that has already been formed

Now, most people here would be thinking of Guide Dogs who assist the blind and the partially sighted; or maybe Hearing Dogs for those who are deaf; or possibly Collie Dogs rounding sheep into their pens; or perhaps Sniffer Dogs helping the police find people who've gone missing; or even ferocious Watch Dogs guarding large stately mansions.

However, Doug has an equally important, but very different, job that he knows is

very special.

He is a Therapy Dog.

ferocious = Aggressive and fierce
therapy = Helpful and comforting treatment

Being of a very well-intentioned nature, he is of the most perfect disposition for such a role where he is to spend every day being good and kind to others.

Doug didn't actually attend college to train for this fine profession, of which he is so proud, but he did have to pass various assessments to confirm his impeccable GOOD nature and suitability for this role. His consultations with a qualified vet assured everyone that his amenable temperament was just PERFECT for his job as a Therapy Dog. He was then able to wear his very special uniform. This makes him feel right and justly proud.

Yey!

disposition = Character
impeccable = Perfect
amenable = Friendly and accommodating

Doug wears this smart uniform for IMPORTANT official engagements such as school assemblies and open days. And, one **very** sad day, Doug wore this uniform for a **special** friend's funeral. During Doug's hospital visits, it had been **really** sad to see his dear friend become so poorly. Doug often remembers this friend with **great** fondness. He does miss his old friend now that he's gone.

Sometimes, Doug is invited to school concerts too. He LOVES to receive such SPECIAL invitations. At one of his schools (he is luckier than most and actually attends several), Doug even has his own stall at their annual summer fayre where he offers opportunities to be photographed for a very small and manageable fee.

He LOVES school trips too. Doug just **adores** being out and about, experiencing somewhere different and learning something new that he would never have known before.

BUCKINGHAM PALACE

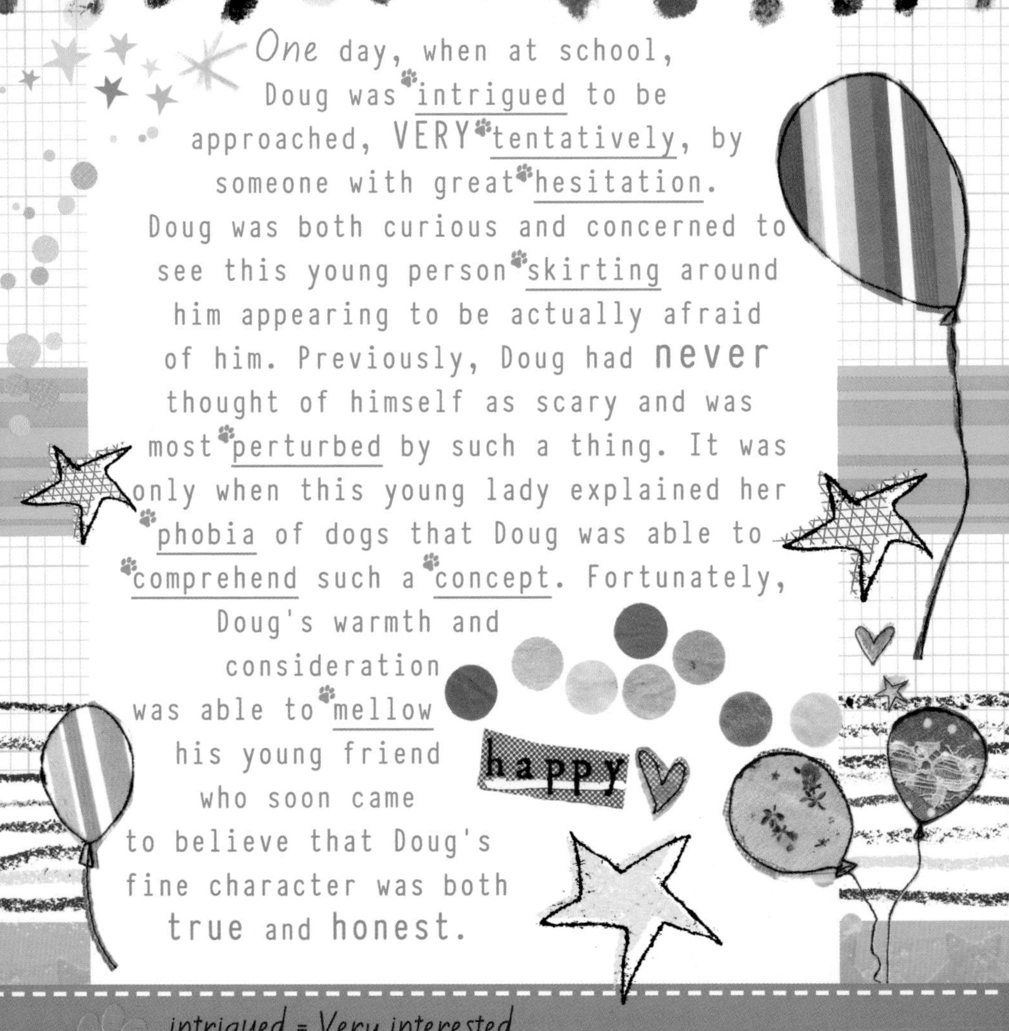

One day, when at school, Doug was intrigued to be approached, VERY tentatively, by someone with great hesitation. Doug was both curious and concerned to see this young person skirting around him appearing to be actually afraid of him. Previously, Doug had **never** thought of himself as scary and was most perturbed by such a thing. It was only when this young lady explained her phobia of dogs that Doug was able to comprehend such a concept. Fortunately, Doug's warmth and consideration was able to mellow his young friend who soon came to believe that Doug's fine character was both **true** and **honest**.

intrigued = Very interested
tentatively = Carefully
hesitation = Uncertainty
skirting = Moving around an edge
perturbed = Troubled
phobia = Great fear
comprehend = Understand
concept = General idea
mellow = Relax

Their time together was **enjoyed** and in no time at all the young lady was able to satisfy herself that any dog she met on her daily travels was quite likely to be just Doug the Pug with longer legs, or bigger ears, or perhaps a longer nose and so on.

This was comforting for the girl, and her family too, as they no longer needed to worry that they might encounter a dog while out at leisure. It was **wonderful** for Doug to see how **confident** and tall his young friend appeared now that her phobia had been addressed and dogs were no longer seen as quite so fearsome.

encounter = Meet by chance

Now, Doug the Pug is a particularly quiet little chap. He rarely barks and most certainly never growls. Doug doesn't feel he needs to use his voice and always seems to manage to make himself understood quite perfectly. Communicating with others can be done in SO many ways - often with the wag of his curly little piggy tail - or the raise of a hairy eyebrow - or the amusing tilt of his wrinkly little scrunched-up face.

Sometimes, if Doug is feeling really sad or worried, his little cinnamon twist of a tail completely unravels and falls quite straight. His sweet velvety ears drop too. This happens during Doug's saddest moments when perhaps a little person appears to be unhappy or he hears a child cry. It can clearly be seen how this breaks Doug's little heart without him saying a word.

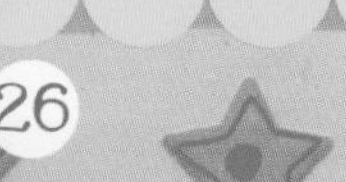

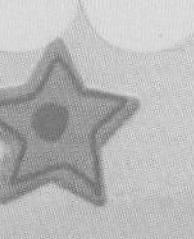

One of Doug's VERY **special** little friends has no voice. This young man fruitfully communicates with others through sign language. He kindly took it upon himself to teach Doug sign language too. It must be said that Doug didn't really get on very well at all with the days of the week but this clever young man successfully taught Doug to sit, stay and come.

This was **such** a FUN game that they were able to share together without saying a word.

fruitfully = Successfully

sign language = Talking to people, using hand signals, body movements and facial expressions instead of voice

It will come as no surprise to hear that Doug is also a real fan of good little people receiving positive recognition for their good work. He treasures seeing how well they are all progressing. Appreciating marvellous pieces of work, displayed for ALL to see, makes Doug burst with pride for those who have achieved so well.

Sometimes, those who take Doug to see their work have incredibly challenging journeys even for seemingly short distances. Some find walking is such hard work that they seek the aid of a walking frame or wheelchair. Doug then happily trots alongside at a pace to suit.

It is then a pleasure for Doug to reward his young friends with a shared story and snuggle on the sofa for such a fine accomplishment.

accomplishment = Something done well

And then there are those who find it just TOO tricky to sit still, listen carefully and think clever thoughts ALL at the same time without annoying the little person sitting next to them. TOO much noise, TOO many people, and TOO many questions coming down on them like hailstones falling from the sky make some of Doug's young friends feel as if the sky itself is falling down. But, placing a kind hand firmly on Doug's soft warm back, whilst twiddling his sweet velvety ears, is found to be the most PERFECT thing to help concentrate and think those clever thoughts.

And there are times when some of Doug's fine young companions can appear to fill up with such incredible crossness that they really do look as if they might actually burst. Often, taking Doug for a quiet wander round the playground in the fresh air and dappled shade can sort things out just perfectly.

And, in what seems like the blink of an eye, everything can be back to normal with those troubles melted away.

Sadly, there are some of Doug's dear friends who can appear full of sorrow. Doug aches enormously for those feeling so lost and empty. He understands that being a true friend can often mean just being there, listening, without the need to say anything at all. And that's exactly what he then does.

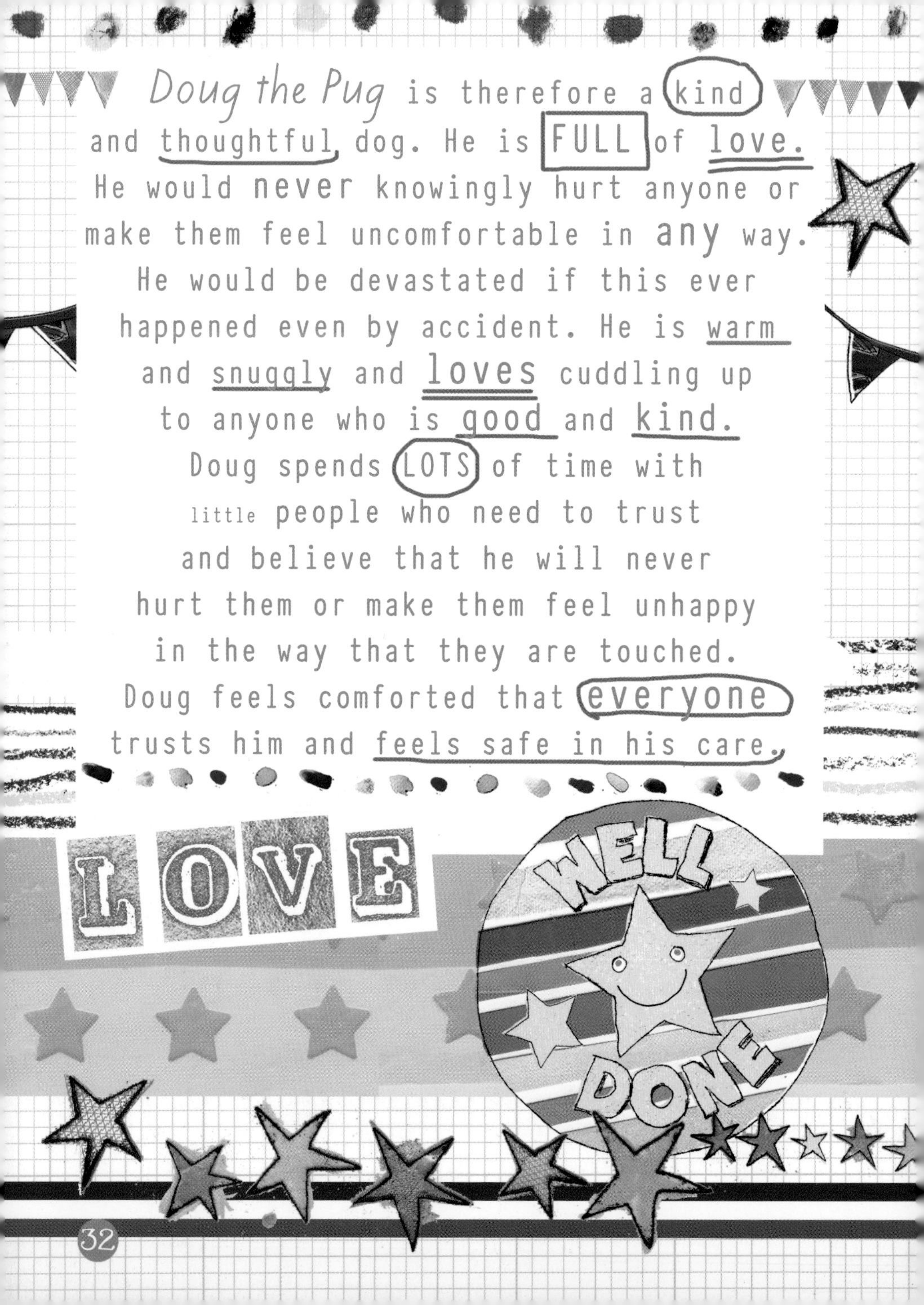

Doug the Pug is therefore a kind and thoughtful dog. He is FULL of love. He would **never** knowingly hurt anyone or make them feel uncomfortable in **any** way. He would be devastated if this ever happened even by accident. He is warm and snuggly and **loves** cuddling up to anyone who is **good** and **kind**. Doug spends LOTS of time with little people who need to trust and believe that he will never hurt them or make them feel unhappy in the way that they are touched. Doug feels comforted that **everyone** trusts him and feels safe in his care.

Because he is so very sweet natured, and also rather round and snuggly, almost everyone who meets Doug thinks he is a real treasure. And so he is. Perhaps even, as some would say, a national treasure.

He is particularly gifted at enabling people to realise they ALL have something quite wonderful to offer. Which of course they always do.

Our lovely Doug the Pug is brave too. He's NOT even scared when he hears of the **big bad** wolf who chased that lovely little girl in the red cape when she was on her way to see her granny. He suspects that this was also the same wolf who terrorised the three little pigs, who had just left their mummy the week before, but cannot really prove that.

Anyway, he knows these are all just pretend stories and that's why he's not scared.
Not scared at ALL.
hello Doug!

Doug so clearly LOVES people (and cats) and he also LOVES stories, so it is quite sad for Doug to find that some people, for a short while, lose their LOVE of books and the fabulous stories they ALL have inside them.

So, it is with immeasurable joy that Doug the Pug finds he is also what is known as a Reading Dog.

immeasurable = So great you can't put a number on it

Quite **wonderful**, in fact. Doug never interrupts, or corrects, his reader and always allows a story to be told in the way its teller likes it best.

His most PERFECT time **ever** is spent cuddled up with a book and a **delightful** person to share it with.

Now, gifted and talented as we know he is, Doug the Pug is not actually able to decipher all of those jumbled-up letters and turn them into words for himself. He needs a clever little person to do that for him.

decipher = Make out, understand the meaning of

It is then that he sometimes takes to closing his eyes, so that he may envisage the **wonderful** tale being shared with him. **Especially** so when there are no pictures on the page to **enjoy**.

And purring too. Pugs do unquestionably purr. It's a **wonderful** little snorty sound that people who know no better can often mistake for snoring. How rude those people must feel Doug is. He would be horrified.

Doug's working days are **FULL** to the brim with **kind, loving** little people reading him stories, enabling him to access **ALL** the FABULOUS tales within the covers of a book.

Doug could never do that for himself.

envisage = See as a picture

So, for Doug the Pug, going to school is the best thing in the world and it is without doubt one of his most favourite places to be.

THE END

If you've got this far, then you've probably finished reading Doug's story already. If that's so, we really do hope you enjoyed it!

This section is one that you could read by yourself, or with friends, or an interested adult. Sometimes, reading with others can help towards making things more interesting. Looking at the areas of further learning, you might create quite a different mix of ideas if you share them out loud with a friend.

If you fancy thinking about things a little deeper – I have added four extra sections here for you to think about Doug's tale in a little more depth.

1. One is about looking at "developing social and emotional understanding" where you can think about feelings and behaviours that influence how we all relate to each other.

2. Next is the "empathetic learning" section where you can discuss the issues above and reflect upon what you care about and why.

3. The next bit is called "extension work and consolidation". Here you can think about the work that Doug enjoys and also that of other working animals while looking at the sort of work they do. You can also find out here about organisations that help us to help animals and other organisations that help animals to help us.

4. The last bit is called "playing with words". This section gives a few ideas as to how you might use Doug's story to help you with your literacy work.

1. Developing social and emotional understanding

If you'd like to reflect upon some of Doug's views and opinions, the bits below will help you to have a good think about the things that he cares about.

You might find that you care about the same things too – you might find that you don't! Having a good think about why people feel and behave as they do can be very interesting. And, this also helps us work towards getting along with others very nicely indeed.

These areas of insight, taken from Doug's book, have been used to create points for discussion in the empathetic learning section below.

- Appearances can be deceptive – never judge a book by its cover.
- Is it really cool to be cool?
- Be true to yourself.
- It's ok to be different.
- Be happy with who and what you are.
- Be kind. Being kind makes us (and others) happy.
- Nobody's perfect.
- Developing and recognising a conscience.
- Acknowledging consequences of behaviours.
- Have the confidence to choose your friends for yourself.
- Be proud of what you stand for.
- Sickness and death – losing someone special.
- Enjoy experiencing something different and learning something new.
- Managing and working with fears.
- Varying methods of communicating with others.
- Reading positive and negative body language.
- Understanding emotions.
- Enjoy sharing praise and recognition.
- Varying mobility difficulties.
- Attention deficit.
- Anger management.
- Acknowledging feelings of sorrow.
- Positive/negative physical contact.
- Believing we all have something wonderful to offer.
- The concept of real versus pretend and consequential fears.
- Re-learn a love of learning in a safe non-threatening environment.
- The need to work with others to achieve something together.
- Misunderstanding the behaviour of others.
- The human-animal bond.
- Valuing and respecting all life.

2. Empathetic learning

It is sometimes said that one must never judge by appearances. Why do you think this is? Do you agree? Do you think this could apply to people/dogs/books/places? In what way do you think it would? There is an old saying, "never judge a book by its cover". Can you say what this means and why? Think about how it could apply to someone you know, by the way they dress, and how we might judge them unfairly because of this.

Do you think that you have to be "cool" to be "cool"? Should being "cool" really matter at all? Doug is happiest being "who he is" – can you be accepting of who you (and others) really are?

Joanna Lumley, the lovely actress and supporter of many tremendously good causes, wrote Doug the kind message on the back of his book. She has said that every day she tries to make life better for someone. Doug feels totally bewildered by those who choose not to be kind. Think of someone you know who might need a little kindness. How could you brighten their day? Remember, even very small acts of kindness can make an enormous difference to anyone's life. Being kind feels good too!

What qualities do you think Doug admires in himself and others?

Reflect upon your good qualities and why you are proud of them.

Discuss those qualities of which you are not so proud. You might find this one more difficult!

Do you ever feel the presence of your own little Jiminy Cricket? Can you think of an example to illustrate this? What do you think Doug's Jiminy Cricket was trying to tell him? Did he listen? Was there a consequence to ignoring such advice?

Doug believes personal differences should be celebrated. Do you? Why do you think this?

Doug likes to be warm and dry. What fine things in life do you enjoy? Do you ever think you might take these things for granted? Think of others who aren't able to enjoy the basic things we assume will be part of our everyday life. What are you thankful for?

Doug strongly dislikes the rain. What strong dislikes do you have? How do you manage dealing with your strong dislikes without upsetting other people or causing a big fuss?

Doug happily chooses his friends for himself. Is it right that other people might tell you who your friends should be? What makes you feel this way?

Doug is proud to wear his Pets As Therapy uniform. Do you wear anything that makes you feel proud? Does it make you feel you belong somewhere special - such as your school, a sports team, Cubs or Brownies? Maybe you wear an important badge given in recognition of good work or a particular achievement? Perhaps you wear something special to represent your cultural heritage or your faith?

Doug's special friend died after being very poorly. Doug still misses him. It is very difficult visiting someone who is not going to get better. Doug was a good friend to visit him when he was sick. Do you think that is a comfort to Doug when he remembers the special times he shared with his old friend?

Doug loves experiencing somewhere different and learning something new. Do you?

Thinking of Doug's young friend who had a phobia of dogs, are you fearful of anything? Do you know why? Can you think of a way that you might overcome those fears? Doug was able to persuade his young friend that all dogs were really just like him but with longer legs or bigger ears or a longer nose! That changed her life and that of her family – it was a great strategy to adopt.

When Doug is sad, his sweet velvety ears drop and his little cinnamon twist of a tail falls quite straight. When he is happy, this little twist of a tail is a lovely tight curl and his ears are pert. Think of people's body language and how they hold themselves when they are happy – people then stand and sit very differently when they are sad or cross or scared. Have a little look at the people around you and see if you think you can tell how they're feeling. Without using your voice, practise communicating these feelings to those around you and see if they can guess the emotion you are trying to portray.

Feeling the comfort of stroking an animal is said to reduce blood pressure and relieve stress. Doug's young friends feel calm and relaxed when they are with him. What do you like to do to relax and feel calm?

Some of Doug's young friends, when feeling things are a bit much for them, like to take Doug for a walk in the dappled shade and fresh air of the playground. What calming things can you do for yourself to avoid feeling overwhelmed?

Doug understands that being a true friend can often mean just being there, listening, sometimes without even needing to say anything at all. What can you do to be a good friend to someone who is feeling lonely or sad?

Those who work with Doug need to trust and believe that he will never hurt them or make them feel unhappy in the way that they are touched. Can you think why this might be?

Doug believes that we all have something wonderful to offer. Think of your family, friends and classmates and what good things they all have to offer.

Doug is a wonderful Reading Dog and loves his work but recognises that he could not do this without the help of a clever little person. What things do you enjoy doing that you could not manage alone? Who helps you? Do you think you make a good team together?

School is one of Doug's favourite places. Where are your favourite places? What makes them special?

People can develop a very special bond with their companion animal (this is another term for a pet). These animals are said to offer unconditional love and are non-judgemental – can you explain what this means and why it is important to us?

It is said that people benefit physically, emotionally and socially from living with and caring for companion animals. Can you think why this would be? Perhaps thinking about Doug and the work he does might help you.

Sharing responsibility for the care of a companion animal like Doug is said to help develop respect and value for all life. Do you agree?

If you were Doug, who would you like to help next? Why? How do you think you would do this?

3. Extension work and consolidation

Design a new uniform for Doug. What do you think he would like to wear? A coat, a hat? Boots to wear in the rain?

Draw a picture of the things that help you when you're feeling down – think of the things that help to make you feel better and stop you from feeling sad.

Thinking about the work of Guide Dogs for the Blind, take turns to lead a friend, who is blindfolded, and steer them carefully around obstacles. Ask them if you made them feel safe.

Make a list of all the working dogs you can think of and what they do. Search and Rescue, Guide Dogs, Hearing Dogs, Assistance Dogs, Detection Dogs, Military Dogs, Police Dogs, Therapy Dogs, Farm Dogs, Hunting Dogs ...

Discuss what breed of dog is most suitable for each role and whether this matters. Discuss the people they help and how they do this. Are they specific to a country or region? For example, a Husky uses snow to aid the pulling of a sledge.

Dogs aren't the only animals used in therapy! In the Ukraine, wounded soldiers have therapeutic sessions in the water with dolphins; a man in Minnesota has a therapy pig, called Carol, who is helping him after skull and back fractures; a nursing home in Florida has a therapy tortoise, called Shelly, who was brought in to cheer people up – and there is a pony, called Luna, who brings a sense of well-being to children in hospital! Perhaps you could do some research to find your most interesting therapy animal and discover what they do to help people feel better.

Discuss other working animals such as farm, hunting, rodeo, circus and zoo animals. Discuss personal opinions on such roles. Justify your answers while understanding and appreciating that there may be no right and wrong answers. Respect and listen to the views of others even if you disagree with them.

Discuss working animals over time. Think about the tasks these animals once carried out and if they still do these jobs today. For example, there was a breed of dog in the 1800s called a Turnspit (which no longer exists) – this dog used to run in a large wooden wheel (like a hamster) to turn a crank that turned a spit for cooking. This dog also ran on a treadmill to provide power before electricity was invented.

Think of the skills and qualities that working animals need for their various roles (elephants, cattle, horses, dogs...). Discuss such things as - fast, strong, patient, affectionate, agile, resilient to weather conditions and deprivation, scenting ability...

Reflecting on the work of these animals, use your strength to push, pull, lift and drag.

Read about the different organisations that help animals: Royal Society for the Prevention of Cruelty to Animals; RSPCA - (www.rspca.org.uk), World Wildlife Fund; WWF - (www.wwf.org.uk), Blue Cross (www.bluecross.org.uk), World Animal Protection (www.worldanimalprotection.org.uk), Dog Trust (www.dogtrust.org.uk), International Fund for Animal Welfare (www.ifaw.org). Do you know of any others?

Think about organisations that help animals to help us. For example, Pets As Therapy (PAT) (www.petsastherapy.org), Guide Dogs for the Blind (www.guidedogs.org.uk), Hearing Dogs for Deaf People (www.hearingdogs.org.uk), Medical Detection Dogs (www.medicaldetectiondogs.org.uk), Canine Partners (www.caninepartners.org.uk). Can you think of others?

The Pets As Therapy website (www.petsastherapy.org) has a lot of really good information leaflets that you can download if you would like a greater understanding of Doug the Pug's work and that of other companion animals like him.

The Society for Companion Animal Studies (SCAS) has a really useful website too (www.scas.org.uk) which is very informative and easy to negotiate. If you would like to look into this sort of work at a deeper level, you can read all about the human-animal bond and animal assisted intervention (AAI) on their site.

The American website, HABRI (which stands for Human Animal Bond Research Initiative Foundation) makes for very interesting reading too (www.habricentral.org). HABRI produce a newsletter, via email, which you might like to subscribe to and read.

4. Playing with words

Discuss, or role play, the meanings of words used in Doug's story.

You could use words from the glossary too – this is on the bottom of each page in Doug's story and tells you the meanings of any tricky words that might be new to you.

Perhaps look at words that have the opposite meaning to those that you find. Words of opposite meaning are known as antonyms.

Using a thesaurus, you could re-write some of the sentences by replacing words with those that have a similar meaning. Words that have similar meanings are called synonyms.

Perhaps you could write your own short story using words that are new to you. A dictionary or thesaurus will help you. Design your own glossary in the way that you'd like to see it presented.

An idiom is a phrase not immediately understood from the words contained within it. This is because the phrase also has another meaning taken from its individual words. For example: "It's raining cats and dogs". That phrase is an idiom. It suggests that cats and dogs are actually falling from the sky! But, we understand this to mean that it is just raining really hard.

In our story, it is said that Doug is rather a traditional sort and this makes him feel a little out of things at times – "like a square peg in a round hole". That phrase is also an idiom. Can you think what this means and why? Perhaps you can see how a square peg in a round hole wouldn't quite fit into place – a little like Doug feels about himself, as a traditional sort in a modern world. Look at other idioms (not in Doug's story) and see if you can work out their meanings – "a fish out of water", "the icing on the cake", "a bull in a china shop", "a wolf in sheep's clothing", "hold your horses", "head over heels", "never judge a book by its cover". Some are positive and some are negative in their meaning. Can you see why? Can you think of any other idioms? Perhaps you could make two lists – positive and negative. Maybe you could make up your own!

Homophones are words that sound the same but have different meanings and spellings. Looking at the title of Doug's book, "Doug the Pug – A Working Dog's Tale", can you see a homophone? If we take the word "Tale" and replace it with the word "tail" it actually still makes sense but gives the story a different meaning altogether! Sometimes, this is called "a play on words". If we use the homophone "Doug" and pair it with "dug", it doesn't really make sense at all. Can you think of any other homophones? These ones aren't in Doug's story but might help you to think of some yourself: pair/pear, sew/sow/so, week/weak, aloud/allowed, mail/male, son/sun, cheap/cheep, hoarse/horse. Perhaps you could make sentences, containing both homophones, to illustrate their meaning? For example, Doug the Pug dug a hole in the garden to bury his bone. Doug's story is a fun tale where it is said his curly little tail is like a double cinnamon twist!

Perhaps you would like to make a "Doug" word search, quiz or crossword. Maybe you could make a word cross? A word cross is made up of two odd-letter words which both contain the same letter in the middle. One is written horizontally (sideways) and the other vertically (up and down), with the common letter positioned centrally to both words as they cross. Using words from Doug's book, I created a word cross containing five letters – style/loyal. I then made another, using nine letters – favourite/encounter.

Choose a book that you would like to read to Doug. Write a review as to why you think Doug would like it and also why you would particularly enjoy reading it to him.

Books, or pieces of writing, can be split into two types – fiction (which is a made-up story) and non-fiction (informational writing which has been based on true facts). All books, whatever their type, can be split further into categories called 'genres'. Think of the books you enjoy and list them as to which category they fall into, for example science fiction, action and adventure, romance, horror, poetry, biography, encyclopedia, journal, etc. Can you think of others? Perhaps even split the genre further! There are many types of poetry – here are a few that you might have come across already: acrostic, haiku, limerick, riddle …

"Doug The Pug – A Working Dog's Tale" is based on real-life experiences that have actually happened in Doug's working life. Because of this, Doug's book is an authentic, but discreet, piece of creative non-fiction. Creative non-fiction is a genre of writing where the text is considered to be factually correct, but is written in a style that reads like fiction (a made-up story). Doug's story is "discreet" because there is no way of knowing the identity of Doug's young friends, or where it is that he sees them. Perhaps you could use an article from your local paper to create a piece of creative non-fiction of your own – or maybe use something that has happened in your own life or that of your family. But, please be discreet – it would be awful to offend someone!

A little bit about Doug the Pug and me

Doug the Pug is a Pug. He is five years old and I am more than ten times that! We both live together in Buckinghamshire and in London with our human and animal families.

Doug and I work together (voluntarily) through a UK charity called Pets As Therapy. For us to earn our registration with Pets As Therapy, Doug had to be thoroughly assessed by a qualified and certified vet. PAT (short for Pets As Therapy) needed to be assured of Doug's impeccable good nature and his reliable disposition. Absolute confirmation was needed that Doug would never react negatively to any inappropriate behaviours, actions or sounds coming his way. He needed to be trusted fully at all times. And, as Doug's owner, I had to have several references taken up too and police checks completed to make sure that people were absolutely safe with both of us.

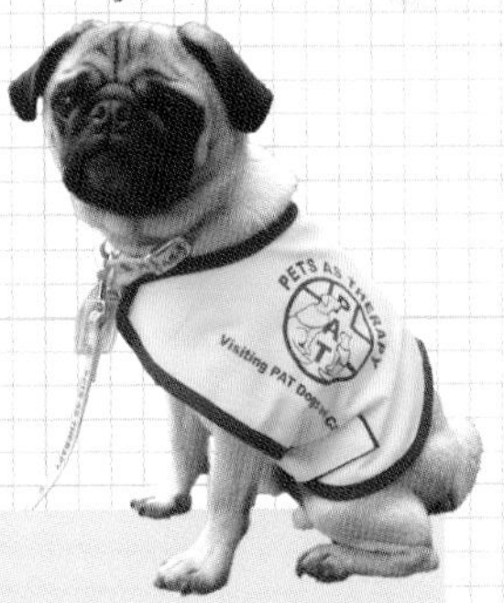

As PAT stands for Pets As Therapy, dogs like Doug are sometimes known as 'pat' dogs. It's because of this that some people think that I take Doug in to schools, hospitals and care homes just to be patted. Sometimes, that is actually just what some volunteers like to do – but others, like Doug and me, prefer to work with people who need a little more support or intervention in their learning or care.

Doug and I come across a wide and varied range of difficulties that face our fine friends. Before he and I worked together, I taught literacy and numeracy to those with learning differences and worked on a positive behaviour analysis programme with children on the autistic spectrum. So, I'm quite well placed to manage the Doug/Cate combo. The main aim, close to our hearts, is that those we work with secure a love of learning in a safe and happy environment. Many adults working through PAT don't have my background but they are still able to make a really big difference.

Doug loves his voluntary work, as I do too. Although seen by many as purely altruistic (kindly and helpful in a charitable way), helping others is said to improve health, happiness and longevity (long life) – so, it really is quite wonderful that such kindness shown to others is of enormous benefit to us all.

Cate XX   Doug XX

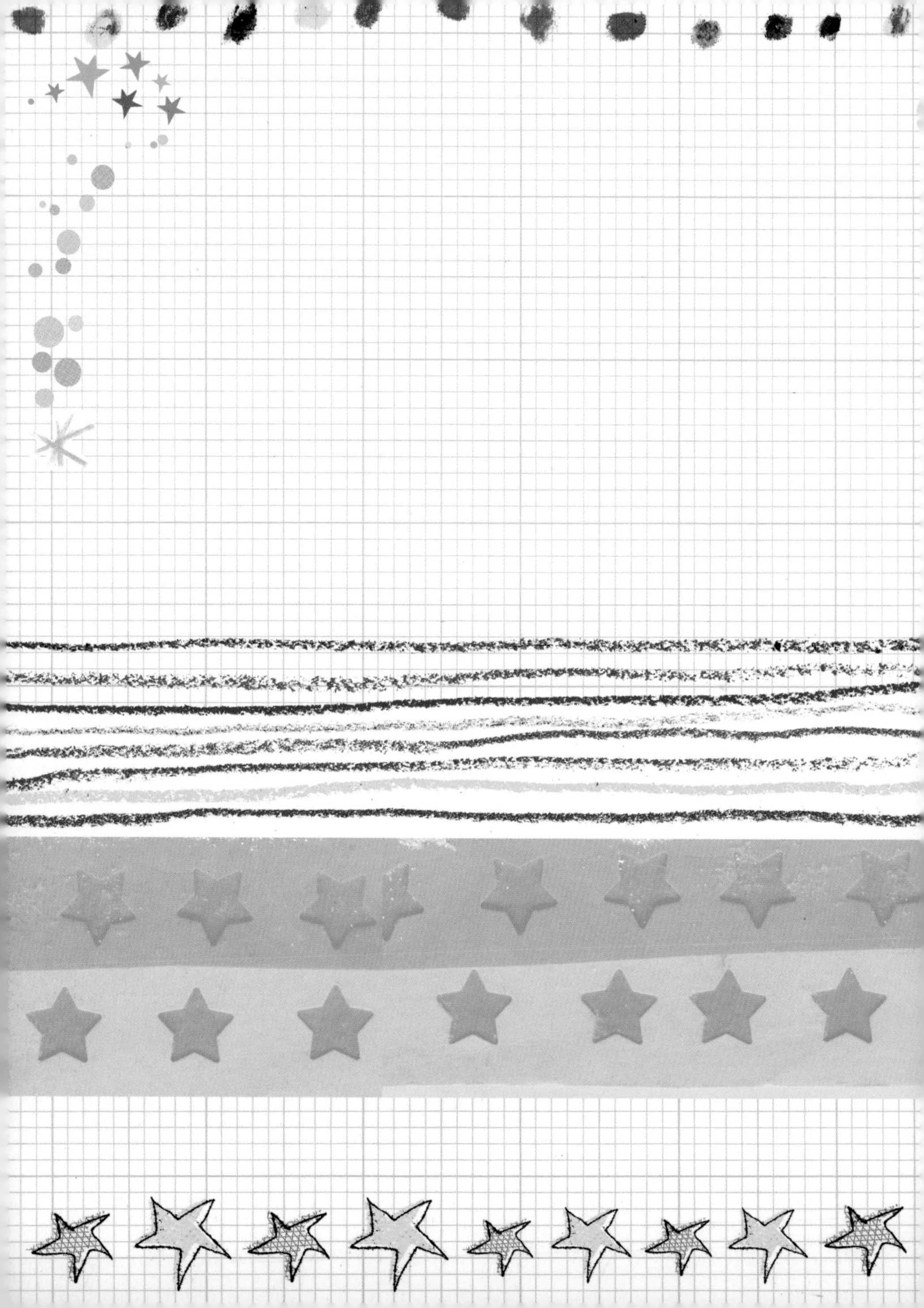